WHODUNITS?™

The Case of the Missing Lettuce

Written by Jack Long

Illustrated by Leonard Shortall

Modern Publishing
A Division of Unisystems, Inc.
New York, New York 10022

TO AMANDA AND
STEPHEN - SHORTALL
L. S.

TO MY GRANDCHILD
NICHOLAS
C.D.L.

TO NINA AND JACK
RIESMAN
J. L.

Published by Modern Publishing,
a division of Unisystems, Inc.

Copyright © 1989 by Carlo DeLucia

TM—WHODUNITS? Mystery Storybooks is a trademark of Modern
Publishing, a division of Unisystems, Inc.

®—Honey Bear Books is a trademark of Honey Bear
Productions, Inc., and is registered in the U.S. Patent and
Trademark Office.

Printed in Belgium

TABLE OF CONTENTS

Chapter One
The First Clue

Betty Beaver and Perry Possum were
having lunch in their new detective agency when
Robert Rabbit rushed through the door.

"Betty, Perry, come quickly," he cried. "Last night, someone stole my head of lettuce!"

"Don't be upset," said Perry. "You have lots of lettuce in your garden."

"No, no!" said Robert. "This was a very special lettuce head. You must find it!"

Betty and Perry followed Robert to his garden.

"I was growing that lettuce for the County Fair. It was beautiful, and sure to win first prize."

"What's first prize?" asked Perry.
"A brand-new, shiny pogo stick," said Robert, "with red tassels on the handles."

GOOD FOREST COUNTY FAIR ▷CONTEST◁
• CARROTS
• CABBAGE
• LETTUCE
• CORN
• TOMATOES
1st PRIZE
POGO STICK ⇨

"See! It's gone!" said Robert.
"Sure is," said Perry.
"Whoever took the lettuce had to have seen it in your garden and plotted how to steal it," said Betty.

"Why don't you write down the names of everyone you showed the lettuce head to," she said.

"Look!" shouted Perry. He pointed to a large leaf of lettuce that was caught on the garden gate.

"Our first clue!" said Betty.

Betty took out her magnifying glass and looked at the leaf.

"I'd better hold on to this," she said. "It may be useful later on."

Betty checked Robert's list.
"We can cross off Barry Blue Jay," she said.
"He would have flown away, not walked
through the gate."

~~Barry Blue Jay~~
Sharpie
Porcupine
Dottie Deer

"Let's go visit the other suspects," said
Betty. "We'll start with Sharpie Porcupine."

Chapter Two
Asking Questions

Betty, Perry, and Robert walked to Sharpie Porcupine's house.

S. PORCUPINE

Sharpie was inside, brushing his quills.

"We've come to ask you a few questions,
Sharpie," said Betty.

"Questions?" cried Sharpie. "Questions?
What sort of questions?" His quills stood up
on end.

"Where were you last night?" asked Perry.

"I went to my sister's birthday party," said
Sharpie.
"Were you there all night?" asked Betty.

"Yes," said Sharpie. "I slept over, too. The party was over late and it was too dark to walk home."

"That's all we needed to know," said Betty. "Thank you very much."

Betty, Perry, and Robert left Sharpie's
house.

"We can cross Sharpie off the list," said Betty. "He was with his family all night."

"Who's next on the list?" asked Perry.

"Dottie Deer," said Robert.

Dottie was outside, lying in the shade of a tree, watching her children play.

"Hello, Dottie," said Betty. "Do you have time to answer a few questions for us?"

"Certainly," said Dottie. "Let's go inside. Come on, children!" she called.

"Where were you last night?" asked Perry,
as they all sat down in Dottie's living room.
"I was here," said Dottie.
"Any witnesses to that?" asked Perry.
Dottie looked confused.

"He means, did anyone see you here?"
explained Betty.

"Oh, yes," said Dottie. "The mayor. She had
dinner with us."

"The mayor!" exclaimed Robert, Perry and Betty.

"Yes," said Dottie. "She had asked me to be the Good Forest School crossing guard next year. She came over to tell me about the job and give me the uniform and the sign."

"Congratulations," said Betty, as they all
went back outside. "I know you will be a good
crossing guard."

36

Betty, Perry, and Robert smiled as they watched Dottie's children line up to help their mother practice for September.

"You certainly can't have a better witness than the mayor," said Betty, as they left Dottie's house. "Dottie gets crossed off the list, too."

"That leaves only one suspect," said Perry.
"Are we going to go visit him?"

"No," said Betty. "I have a better idea."

And she led the way to the County Fair.

Chapter Three
At the Fair

Betty, Perry, and Robert headed for the tent
where the lettuces were being judged.
"There it is!" cried Robert. "There is my
beautiful lettuce head!"

He rushed over to read the card pinned to the lettuce. It said:

This Lovely Lettuce, Perfect in Every Way, Was Grown by Sly Fox in his Private Garden.

"It was not!" shouted Robert angrily. "I grew it, not Sly!"

Perry looked at Betty.

"What are we going to do?" he asked.

"Wait and see," said Betty.

Just then, the judge came over. He looked
at the lettuce and read the card.

"Well," he announced, "it certainly is a lovely lettuce, but it is *not* perfect. There seems to be a large leaf missing from it."

Betty stepped forward.
"I think this is what's missing," she said,
"and here is the card that belongs on the lettuce head."

"This head of lettuce was grown by Robert
Rabbit," read the judge.

The judge put the leaf back on the lettuce.
"Perfect!" he cried.

50

"Mr. Rabbit's lettuce wins the first prize!" announced the judge. "This brand-new, shiny pogo stick!"

"With red tassels!" exclaimed Robert happily.

While everyone gathered around to
congratulate Robert, Betty and Perry left the
lettuce stand, and headed towards the entrance.

They caught Sly Fox trying to sneak away.

"Shame on you!" said Betty. "Stealing
Robert's lettuce! Why did you do it?"

"Because of the prize," said Sly Fox. "I always wanted a pogo stick. Robert doesn't need one! He's a rabbit, and hops and jumps everywhere. It's not fair!"

"That's not a good reason," said Betty. "Robert worked hard. He deserves his prize. If you want a pogo stick, you will have to earn it in an honest way."

"If you help me weed my garden," said
Robert, "I'll share my pogo stick with you."

Robert Rabbit and Sly Fox shook hands.

"Another case solved," said Betty and Perry happily.

"I'm hungry," said Perry. "We never got to finish lunch."

"Then let's get some popcorn," said Betty, "and go for a ride on the ferris wheel."

And they did.